LITTLE MOAR
AND THE MOON

Published by Inhabit Media Inc.
www.inhabitmedia.com

Inhabit Media Inc. (Iqaluit) P.O. Box 11125, Iqaluit, Nunavut, X0A 1H0
(Toronto) 191 Eglinton Avenue East, Suite 301, Toronto, Ontario, M4P 1K1

Editors: Neil Christopher and Kelly Ward
Art director: Danny Christopher

This project was made possible in part by the Government of Canada.

We acknowledge the support of the Canada Council for the Arts for our publishing program.

Library and Archives Canada Cataloguing in Publication

Title: Little Moar and the moon / by Roselynn Akulukjuk ; illustrated by Jazmine Gubbe.
Names: Akulukjuk, Roselynn, author. | Gubbe, Jazmine, illustrator.
Identifiers: Canadiana 20210217081 | ISBN 9781772272994 (hardcover)
Subjects: LCGFT: Picture books.
Classification: LCC PS8601.K86 L58 2021 | DDC jC813/.6—dc23

Printed in Canada

Canadä Canada Council   Conseil des Arts
        for the Arts   du Canada

TLE MOAR AND THE MOON

by Roselynn Akulukjuk

illustrated by Jazmine Gubbe

INHABIT MEDIA

IQALUIT · TORONTO

In the fall, little Moar and his friends were playing baseball after school.

He enjoyed playing outside with friends during this time of the year, but it was also the time of the year when the daylight didn't last very long.

Little Moar was afraid of the moon. Whenever he looked at the moon, he saw a face. The face looked like it was giving him a half-smile, and that scared him.

"I can't play too long. I have to go home before it gets dark," little Moar said to his friends.

He batted one last time. Then he told his friends that he had to go. He suggested they play again tomorrow after school.

Little Moar looked up at the sky. He noticed that it was a shade darker than the last time he had looked up.

On his way home, little Moar saw his other friends playing tag. It looked like they were having a lot of fun.

"Hey Moar, you're missing a fun game of tag. Want to join us?" one of his friends called.

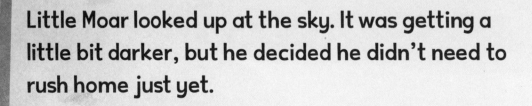

Little Moar looked up at the sky. It was getting a little bit darker, but he decided he didn't need to rush home just yet.

Little Moar started playing tag with his friends. His friends were right. This game of tag was so much fun that little Moar lost track of time.

When little Moar finally looked up at the sky, he realized that it was getting much darker, so he told his friends that he had to go home.

On his way home, little Moar saw his cousin feeding his father's sled dogs. His cousin asked him to help him feed the dogs. There were ten dogs and they had to make sure each dog had about the same amount of food.

Little Moar agreed to help his cousin. Little Moar enjoyed helping out whenever he got a chance. It made him feel good.

But it was getting late . . .

Little Moar looked up at the sky once again and noticed that it was finally dark. The moon had come out, but clouds were covering some parts of the sky, so he could only see the faint glow of the moon behind the clouds.

Little Moar ran inside his cousin's house without finishing with the dogs.

Worried that the clouds would move and the moon would come into view, he watched the sky through the window of the house.

"What are you looking at, *ujuruk*?" asked his uncle.

"I'm waiting for the face in the moon to be covered by clouds so I can run home," replied little Moar. "I like fall, but I don't like that it gets dark so early in the day."

"The face in the moon?" his uncle asked, confused.

"Yes, I see a face when I look at the moon and that scares me," little Moar replied.

Eventually, little Moar saw a big cloud move to cover the moon completely. This was his chance!

He rushed out of his uncle's house and ran as fast as he could toward his own house. As he ran, he stumbled on some soft snow and struggled to keep going.

Little Moar used all his strength to rush through the soft snow. He finally made it to his house. He took off all his winter clothes in a hurry. His parents greeted him and asked why he sounded out of breath.

"I ran home because I didn't want to be outside at the same time as the moon!" little Moar told his mother.

"Why would you be worried about the moon, Moar? It is very far away from Earth and can't hurt you," little Moar's mother said with a smile.

"I am scared of the moon because it has a face! It is always looking right at me with a strange half-smile," explained little Moar.

Little Moar's mother gave him a hug. "The moon doesn't have a face," she told him. "It only looks like it does. It's just a big rock with bumps and shadows on the surface."

Little Moar looked out the window at the moon. Maybe the smile he saw could just be a shadow. But he still didn't like it.

Even if it is far away, thought little Moar, *I am glad I beat the moon home this time!*

Roselynn Akulukjuk was born in Pangnirtung, Nunavut, in the Canadian Arctic. In 2012, Roselynn moved to Toronto to pursue a career in film and attend the Toronto Film School, where she fell in love with being behind the camera. After finishing her studies and working in Toronto, Roselynn returned home to Nunavut, where she began working with Taqqut Productions, an Inuit-owned production company located in the capital of Nunavut, Iqaluit. Part of Roselynn's love of filmmaking is the ability to interview Elders, listen to their traditional stories, and share them with the world. In 2015, Roselynn wrote and directed her first film, the live-action and puppetry short *The Owl and the Lemming*, on which her book by the same title is based. Her film won Best Animation at the 2016 American Indian Film Festival.

Jazmine Gubbe is an illustrator from Ontario currently working in the animation industry. When she is not painting she is hiking, exploring nature, and learning the mysterious local history.

Inuktitut Pronunciation Guide

Note: Capital letters denote the emphasis.

ujuruk	u-JU-ruk	nephew or niece (used when the speaker is the brother of the child's mother)

For more Inuktitut-language resources, visit inhabitmedia.com/inuitnipingit.

INHABIT MEDIA
IQALUIT · TORONTO